MOIRA MILLER

Hamish
and the
Fairy Gifts

Illustrated by Mairi Hedderwick

D1428846

CANONGATE
KELPIES

Also by Moira Miller
Hamish and the Wee Witch

If you enjoyed this Kelpie and would like a free
Kelpie sticker and catalogue please contact:

Customer Services
Canongate Books Ltd
14 High Street
Edinburgh EH1 1TE

First published in Great Britain in 1988
by Methuen Children's Books Ltd
Published in Kelpies 1995

Text Copyright © Moira Miller 1988
Illustrations copyright © Mairi Hedderwick 1988

British Library Cataloguing-in-Publication Data
A catalogue record of this book is available upon request from
the British Library.

ISBN 0 86241 565 9

Printed and bound in Denmark by Norhaven A/S

Contents

Hamish   *page* 5

1 Hamish and the Fairy Bairn   9

2 Hamish and the Seal People   25

3 Hamish and the Bogle   39

4 Hamish and the Green Mist   53

5 Hamish and the Birds   67

6 Hamish and the Fairy Gifts   81

Hamish

The village of Camusbuie lies at the head of a silver sea loch on the west coast of Scotland.

There are three roads leading out of Camusbuie. The broad straight road marches to the south. The rough stony road struggles up the hillside to the Ben of Balvie, and the mountains beyond. But the third road meanders happily through the trees, down along the loch-side where the sun dances on the water, and across a little wooden bridge over the Balvie Burn to a white farmhouse.

The farm belongs to Hamish and Mirren. Together they work in the three green fields that stretch down the hill to the waterside. In summer, Hamish launches his boat to fish the loch, and all year round they are both helped by Hamish's old mother, who lives with them.

'Hamish, you mind and wrap up well when you go out in that boat. It's going to be gey wet later on. Mark my words.'

'Yes, mither,' sighed Hamish, but he went back for his sou'wester, and was glad that he had when the black clouds swept across the bay later that afternoon.

'Mirren, don't forget to chop an apple into the bramble jam this year or it'll never set.'

'Aye, right mother,' sighed Mirren, stirring the jam under the old woman's beady, watchful eye. She added the apple, and the jam set firm and purple as amethyst in the little pots.

She was always right, was the old lady. Somehow she seemed to know more than most people had ever forgotten. She even knew a good deal more than was usual about the Wee Folk and all the mischief they could brew up. Hamish and Mirren used to smile at some of her stories, calling them fairy nonsense, but there came a time when they were very grateful indeed for what she knew.

Hamish

Mither

Mirren

1
Hamish and the Fairy Bairn

It all started one wild night in January. A storm had raged all week, howling round the top of the Ben, and tearing through the trees around the farmhouse, as if to rip them out of the ground. Rain and sleet filled the burn to overflowing, until the water crashed down off the mountainside, roaring like a savage beast.

On the wildest night of all Mirren's baby son was born, and the floodwater of the Balvie Burn washed away the little wooden bridge, leaving the farmhouse cut off from the village.

Neither Hamish nor Mirren cared. She lay happy and cosy in the big bed, cuddling her new baby in his soft knitted shawl. Hamish sat by her side, stroking the baby's soft ginger curls.

'Do you think he'll want to be a farmer or a fisherman, Mirren? Should I make him a wee wheelbarrow or a fishing rod?'

Mirren laughed.

'Bring me his cradle first,' she said. 'I think Torquil will be needing that more than a barrow just now.'

The baby was to be christened Torquil

after Mirren's father, the laird.

Hamish had spent the summer evenings making a sturdy little cradle of fresh sweet-smelling pinewood. Mirren and the old lady had filled it with soft knitted blankets, and for weeks it had stood ready and waiting by the fireside in the kitchen. As Hamish bent to lift it he looked across at his mother who was staring gloomily into the flames.

'What's the matter,' he asked. 'Are you not happy?'

'Och, I'm fair delighted for the pair of you,' she sighed. 'But it's just my wee grandson I'm not sure about. If you had only made that cradle out of rowan wood when I told you, then the Wee Folk. . .'

'That's just havers,' Hamish laughed, 'There's no Wee Folk coming into this house. I'll see to that.'

She sighed, ignoring him. 'And that bairn with the red hair. The King's colour. The very thing they prize the most. I tell you, Hamish, he will not be safe until he is christened in Camusbuie Kirk, and that will not happen as long as the bridge is down.'

'I'll mend the bridge as soon as may be,' said Hamish. 'In the meantime wee

Torquil will be quite safe with Mirren.'

'Hamish! What ever are you thinking of, saying the bairn's name out loud like that. And you standing by the fireplace.' His mother was quite shocked. 'Do you not realise They are up there, round the chimney stack, listening for that very thing so that they can call the wee one to them?' Hamish just shook his head and laughed and took the cradle through to the bedroom.

Late that night Mirren woke up. Wee Torquil was crying for his feed so she stirred the fire in the kitchen to a warm glow and sat in the big chair singing softly to him. As she sang, the wind dropped to a soft moan, and through it came another sound, echoing down the chimney. A strange, sweet music.

'Torquil, Torquil, son of Hamish,
Come away, come away.'

The baby turned towards the fireplace, holding out his tiny hands. Mirren leapt instantly to her feet, bundling him tight and safe in the shawl. The strange, sweet music was all around her, filling the room.

'Mother,' she called banging on the old

13

lady's bedroom door. 'Mother, come quick!'

The old lady padded through to the kitchen in her long white nightdress, pushing her spectacles up on to her nose. She stopped in the doorway suddenly, hearing the tiny voices, and seeing Torquil's bright little eyes turned towards the fire.

'I knew it,' she said. 'They're after the bairn. Havers indeed! You just wait till I have a word with our Hamish. If he had made that cradle out of rowan wood when I told him to, there would have been none of this.'

'Mother, what can we do?' begged Mirren as Torquil began to howl loudly and to wriggle and kick in her arms.

'We'll just have to find a way to stop them coming down that chimney,' said the old lady. She poked about in the basket of dry sticks by the hearth and at last pulled out a little sprig of fir tree, still with the green needles on it.

'A wee trick I learned a while back. This may hold them for a bit.' She pushed the twig through the links of the heavy black iron chain that held the kettle over the flames. The moaning in the chimney changed to an angry howl, then died on the wind.

Over the next few days, the Wee Folk tried all the tricks they knew to sneak in and take away the baby. Hamish's mother went round the cottage and round the cottage searching for ways to stop them.

She unravelled a red ribbon from her best petticoat and tied it around the cradle. Then she sent Hamish out into the storm to cut branches from the rowan tree to nail above the front and back doors of the cottage.

For three days and nights the wind raged and the voices moaned in the chimney. Each night Hamish, Mirren and the old lady took it in turns to sit by the cradle, keeping a wakeful and watchful eye on Torquil. Sometimes the baby would waken and, howling loudly, reach out a little hand towards the door.

'Aye, that bairn has his father's voice, right enough,' said the old lady. 'The noisiest child in Camusbuie, but we must be careful. They're still after him for all that.'

On the third evening the wind died back, there was a glimmer of sunset out

16

over the sea and the black clouds rolled away from the top of the Ben. The weather was lifting and with it the raging water of the burn settled to a thick brown hurlygush.

'I'll mend the bridge in the morning,' yawned Hamish. 'Then we can take wee Torquil down to Camusbuie Kirk for the christening.'

'I'll not be happy until then,' grumbled his mother. She shook her fist up the chimney. 'Away you go, back to your own folk, you little devils!' A tiny giggle floated down to them. 'Impertinent craturs!' she grumbled. 'You be sure and lock up properly tonight, Hamish. I'm away to my bed.'

But Hamish was tired and although he remembered to push the door shut, he forgot to slip the heavy iron bolt into the hasp.

Late that night, when everyone was asleep, the wind suddenly arose in a last furious gust. The door crashed open sending sparks flying up the chimney. The cat flew, squalling, from the hearth-rug and the enamel milk-jug toppled off the table and rolled with a clang across the floor. The old lady struggled out of bed. Hamish jumped up, with Mirren close behind him, and together they managed to slam shut the door against the storm. Only wee Torquil lay peacefully in his cradle by the fire as if nothing had happened.

'Fancy him just sleeping through all that!' said Mirren.

'Aye, just fancy,' said the old lady doubtfully peering into the cradle.

Everything seemed quite normal when Hamish set out early next morning to mend the bridge. But that evening when he returned he found Mirren still sitting by the cradle, looking worried.

'It's very odd,' she whispered. 'He hasn't cried all day.'

'Thank goodness for that,' said Hamish, flopping into a chair. 'Maybe we'll all get some sleep tonight.'

And indeed the baby slept right through until morning when Mirren went to lift him for his feed.

'It's really very odd,' she said. 'His eyes were blue, but they seem to be green now. They do say a baby's eyes change colour sometimes. Is that right, mother?'

'Aye, it can be,' said the old lady, warily.

During the next few days, while Hamish mended the bridge, she and Mirren watched the baby uneasily. He lay, still and silent, and the little bright eyes watched them in a knowing, clever way. At last the old lady, who had been sitting thinking, put down her knitting and studied him closely.

'I'm beginning to wonder if the Wee Folk are maybe away with our Torquil right enough,' she said.

'Oh no, mother, surely not, we were so careful.' Mirren stared at the baby, with his little, bright, green, shining eyes, and grew suddenly uneasy.

'If they had taken him,' she said in horror, 'how could you tell?'

'Oh, that's not so difficult,' said the old lady nodding her head wisely.

She went to the cupboard and brought out a large jar of her home-made jelly, dipped in a little silver spoon and touched it to the baby's lips. He set up such a howling and screeching that the china dogs on the mantelpiece rattled and Hamish, hearing the row from down at the bridge, dropped his hammer and came running.

'I thought as much,' nodded the old

lady. The screaming baby sat up suddenly in the cradle, his tiny face quite purple with fury, and the ginger curls straight up in spikes all over his head. 'That's no human child. They've taken our wee Torquil and left us a fairy bairn in his place.'

'But how can you tell?' wailed Mirren above the din.

'Because a fairy cannot abide the rowan tree, and that was rowan jelly,' said the old lady triumphantly. 'Our wee Torquil loved it. I fed him the odd spoonful – just in case.

'Mither!' protested Hamish, but Mirren stopped him.

'It's just as well she did, Hamish, or we'd never have known. But how are we to get rid of this creature and get our own wee bairn back?'

'I'll soon see to that,' said the old lady. She quickly slipped another spoonful of the jelly into the baby's mouth. He screeched even louder, shot out of the cradle, flew three times round the room in a furious bundle of blankets and out through the open door.

'Follow him, quickly,' she bellowed. 'See where he goes!'

The strange little creature tore up the hillside behind the cottage leaving a trail of blankets and a path scorched through the heather. Hamish and Mirren raced after him, with the old lady puffing up behind them, still clutching the jar of jelly and grumbling to herself.

'If that daft beggar had just listened to me and made the bairn a cradle of rowan wood in the first place. . .'

Up the hillside they raced. Up through the trees, across the shoulder of the Ben, and down into the Fairy Glen where the heather grew thickest and even in the hardest winters the snow melted first. Hamish raced on, following the fairy bairn to a green, grassy mound at the head of the glen. The creature, skirling and shrieking, burrowed into the long grass, with Hamish all set to follow after him.

'STOP THERE!' yelled his mother. 'Have you no sense at all? Listen!'

They stood, panting and breathless, and gradually, as their pounding hearts stilled, the sounds of the glen came to them. The birds were quiet, as if singing in a whisper. The wind through the bracken was soft and above it came another sound, far beneath their feet, deep in the earth. It was the sound of tiny voices arguing, and above them all, the howling, hungry cry of the noisiest baby in Camusbuie.

'It's Torquil,' shouted Mirren gleefully.

'Aye,' said the old lady. 'And I think they've stolen more than they bargained for this time.'

The hungry howls grew even louder, the argument more furious as she marched boldly up to the grassy mound and tapped with her little silver spoon on a stone as if it had been a boiled egg. The voices stopped instantly.

'You thought to steal away my grandson, did you? I hope you're pleased with him,' she shouted. The tiny voices wailed in misery above the baby's howling.

'Please! Please! Please take him away!' they moaned.

'Aye, well I might...' said the old lady. Hamish opened his mouth, but she held up her hand to silence him. 'I might just take him away again. On one condition.'

'Anything. Anything at all,' the fairy voices wailed.

'I'll take him if you will promise my wee grandson the Fairy Hansel – the Wee Folks' gift to a new bairn. Grant him your help whenever he calls on you throughout his life – and we'll say no more about it.

Mirren gasped: 'The Fairy Hansel! They only give that to the son or daughter of a king.'

'And why shouldn't our Torquil have it? He's as fine as any king's bairn, I'm sure.' The old lady raised her voice and shouted again. 'Do you hear me? What do you say?'

Wee Torquil certainly heard her, and bawled louder than ever.

'Anything! Anything you wish. Only take him. Please take him, and with him the Fairy Hansel.'

As the voices died away, the glen whirled around them, the air was filled with a strange whistling music, which faded as the baby's howls grew even louder.

'Torquil!' shouted Mirren, recovering first. Lying at their feet, still wrapped in his knitted shawl, with his little face quite scarlet beneath the ginger curls, lay Torquil. Hamish lifted him gently, and the old lady slipped a spoonful of rowan jelly into his yelling mouth.

'Well, look at that,' said Mirren. 'He's smiling at us.'

'Aye, and no thanks to his stupid big father,' sniffed the old lady, following them down the Glen, back to the farmhouse. 'If you had just listened to me and made the bairn a cradle of rowan wood in the first place . . .'

But neither Hamish, Mirren nor Wee Torquil, sound asleep in his mother's arms, were listening to her.

2
Hamish and the Seal People

Hamish had taken a day away from the farm, and gone fishing. He pushed his wee boat down the rocky beach into the water. Then, rowing out to the mouth of the loch, where the brown hill water met the green sea, he cast his lines and waited. But never a fish did he catch.

Not one.

Through that long hot day the sun glittered on the sea, melting the wind-ripples into a sheet of glass. Hamish baited hook after hook, dropped them over the side and lay back in the sunshine to wait. At last, as the sun was sliding towards the headland in the west he sat up and yawned.

'Ach, it's no use, the fishes must have all gone on their holidays. Time I was away home for my tea.' Slowly, he hauled up the line, hand over hand. Suddenly there was a tug, and the boat rocked violently.

'Mercy on us, whatever have we got here? It must be a whale, I'm thinking.'

He yanked the line hard. It tugged back, pulling him against the side of the

27

boat. For five long minutes he rolled backward and forward, as the sea creature caught on his hook gradually became weaker and weaker.

Hamish gave one last mighty heave — and the line broke.

'Ouch!' He sat down hard in the bottom of the boat, then struggled to his knees in time to see a long, dark, gleaming shape turn and twist in the water. A trail of silver bubbles floated to the surface as it vanished.

'Well, I never,' he gasped, picking himself up. 'That was a real monster I've lost, and my hook as well. No fish for dinner tonight, I doubt.' He settled himself in the boat, fitted the oars in the rowlocks and pulled for the head of the loch and home.

'Help! Help me, fisherman!'

Hamish turned at a shout from the beach. On the sand bar by the mouth of the loch, shadowy against the setting sun, stood a short square man. The golden light gleamed on his thick black hair and on the soft fur jerkin he wore. He was small, but powerful, and his face was brown as a gipsy. Hamish hesitated. But the man demanded help and, stranger or not, he must be given it.

'You must help me, fisherman,' the man called again. His voice was soft, but strangely commanding.

Hamish found himself pulling the boat towards the beach. Unable to resist, he climbed out and pulled it up on to the sand. The man's eyes, watching him, were dark and deep as the ocean.

'Fisherman,' he said softly. 'You have hurt my brother this day. He is mortally wounded, and you alone can help him.'

'Your brother?' Hamish was astonished. 'I would hurt nobody. I am a peaceful man.'

'That is as may be. But nonetheless he is hurt, and by your hand.'

'But I have been fishing,' protested Hamish. 'And saw no man all this long day.'

'No man of your race, perhaps. But you cast your line into our Kingdom, without thought or care, and now my brother is hurt sore. You must come to him.'

The dark man took Hamish by the hand, and led him down the beach towards the edge of the sea. Unable to pull back from the cold strong grip, Hamish shook his head in horror as he found

29

himself dragged into the water.

'No! No, I cannot go with you. I must not.'

The man smiled, his grip stronger than ever.

'Keep by my side, fisherman, and you will come to no harm.' Wading deeper and deeper towards the gold path of the sinking sun, he led Hamish on until the dark water closed over their heads. Only the otters playing on the wet sand saw their last footprints covered by the lapping waves. Only the herring gull, swooping high above, saw their hair, tawny as seaweed, vanish beneath the waves.

Hamish gasped, fighting for breath in the cold water, and then opened his eyes in astonishment. He had swum in the sea often enough before, but this was different. In the enchanted grasp of the Seal Man he felt himself floating, flying almost, in a cool green world where he could see and breathe. Deeper and deeper they twisted and turned. Hamish held tightly to the cold hand in his and allowed himself to be drawn towards the far off glimmering green-silver of the sandy sea bed. Shoals of tiny fish drifted

30

around them, like a shower of raindrops in sunlight. Instantly, as if to a silent command, they darted off, all turning together towards a mound of seaweed-covered rock far beneath.

Around the rock waving fronds of weed reached out as if blown in a gentle breeze. The Seal Man parted them, uncovering the entrance to a dark cave, and drew Hamish in.

In the shifting, flickering light, they were surrounded by black shapes who came and went silently. Hamish turned back, to find that they followed close behind them, blocking the way out of the cave, and still the Seal Man drew him on, gliding through the green water.

'You will come to no harm,' he said. 'So long as you are with me.'

They swam through twisting passageways until Hamish had lost all sense of direction, and came at last to a small chamber, so round and perfect it seemed to have been cut from the rock. A weird shimmering light glowed from an open shell in which lay a pearl, the like of which Hamish had never seen before.

'Man,' he gasped. 'It's the size of a potato, yon thing!'

'Hush, fisherman,' whispered the Seal Man. 'We have come to my brother.'

In the centre of the sandy floor of the cave stood a large flat stone. It was draped with a soft cloak, the edges of which waved in the gently shifting currents, like a living thing. On the cloak there lay a dark figure, as still as death.

'Our chieftain,' said the man. 'And my brother. Please, I beg you, help him.'

Hamish crept closer. The man's thick dark hair floated around his face. On his right arm the shirt was torn, slashed and bloodstained where a fishing hook had been pulled deep into the flesh.

'It is your hook and it is iron,' said the man by his side. 'To us it means certain death and we may not touch it. Only a human may free him.' He held out a small knife, the blade made of pink sea shell.

Around them the dark shadowy figures came closer. As the Seal People gathered about the bed of their chieftain, Hamish could see that they were men and women, old and young, all with the glossy dark hair and eyes of the man by his side.

He knew their stories well enough.

From childhood he had heard his mother tell them so often. Like the Wee Folk, they were of the old enchanted world before the Age of Iron, and that metal spelt death to their charmed lives.

'I see now how I have done your brother hurt,' he said, understanding at last.

Taking the shell knife, he slit the man's sleeve. Slowly and carefully, he cut the hook from the torn flesh, while the others watched. Then he took from his pocket a little pot of salve, which he always carried.

'This is prepared by my mother,' he said. 'And will cure most ills. It is made of seaweed from the shore and self-heal from the hillside.' Gently he rubbed the salve into the wound, and bound it with a frond of the healing seaweed.

'I have done what I can,' he said. 'Now I must return home, for Mirren and my mother will surely be afraid for me, should they find my boat empty on the beach, and my little son will miss his father.'

But the man who had brought him shook his head, for his brother lay unmoving, with his eyes closed.

'No, fisherman, you may not leave without my help and I must be sure that my brother is well. We must wait.' He turned from Hamish and crouched by his brother's side.

Hamish sighed and joined him as the dark figures shifted closer.

Through long hours they waited and watched in the pale light. Around them the Seal People sang softly, a wordless song that rose and fell in his ears like the music of the sea, until, gradually, Hamish fell asleep.

He woke suddenly, at a cry from the man who had fetched him.

'He is awake! My brother is awake, fisherman.'

Stumbling to his feet in a sleepy daze, Hamish saw that the man on the rock lay with his eyes open, watching them.

'Fisherman,' he whispered, 'I have much to blame, but more to thank you for.' Hamish, speechless, shook his head. The man smiled.

'I know of you, fisherman,' he said. 'We have watched you, my people and I. I know that you would hurt no creature willingly. Return now, with my brother, to your own people. But, beware, and heed my warning. Cast no more hooks of iron where my people swim and we may live together peaceably.'

'You have my word and my hand on that,' said Hamish. 'From this time on I will take heed and watch out for you and your people.'

As he reached out to grip the cold hand of the chieftain there came a rushing in his ears. Tossed like a cork in a whirlpool, Hamish found himself struggling in the water, as if he had fallen from the boat. He kicked out and swam alone up towards the light.

As he waded from the sea, the sun still hung, a half-sunk ball of golden fire, spreading its path across the water towards him.

The tide still lapped around his footprints, vanishing into the water from the wet sand. Of the other man's footprints there was no sign.

His little boat lay drawn up on the beach, just as he had left it, and far up the loch, in the blue dusk, Mirren had placed a light in the window of the wee farmhouse.

Hamish blinked and shook his head, looking down at his clothes. They were dry as the dusty summer fields.

'I doubt but I must have been out in the sun too long and fallen asleep,' he said, scratching his head. 'A strange dream that was! Time I was home to Mirren right enough.'

He turned then to push the boat back into the water and found that in his hand he still held the little shell knife of the Seal People, while at his feet lay three fine plump silver mackerel, a gift from the sea.

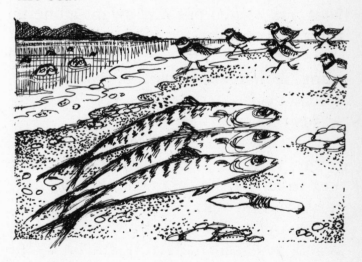

3
Hamish and the Bogle

Everyone was talking down in Camus-buie. Heads nodded and tongues wagged – but always in whispers.

'Did you ever hear the like of it?' said Wee Maggie to the crowd in the village shop.

'Hear it? HEAR it, did you say?' Andy the postman looked around the other customers who stood with their eyes goggling. 'Did I not SEE it for myself?'

'Never!'

'Tell us aboot it.'

'What was it like? Did it have huge flashing eyes like they say?'

'And a wail that turned your blood to ice?'

'Were you not – TERRRRRIFIED?'

'W-e-e-e-e-ll,' said Andy. 'I didna' like it much. It takes a brave man to face a thing like yon. I'll tell you, this was the way of it . . .' They gathered round in fascinated horror as he lowered his voice.

'I was coming home late the other night, round the road by the shore – past the ruined cottage . . .'

Hamish, who had gone into Camusbuie to do some shopping for Mirren, stopped to listen with the others. It seemed that Andy had been walking home alone in the dark, when suddenly, passing the cottage, he heard a noise behind him.

'Hoooo-hoooo! Hoooooo-eeeeech! O-o-o-o-o-h!'

'It was bloodcurdling right enough,' whispered Andy. 'And when I looked round, there was the ghost – a great white bogle, wailing and moaning . . .'

'Aaaaaaah!' They were pop-eyed with excitement in the shop.

' . . . flitting in and out among the trees by the old ruined cottage. I stopped to get a better look at him and, guess what – he vanished clean through the wall.'

'Mercy on us, Andy,' gasped Wee Maggie behind the counter. 'That's enough to give anyone the heebie-jeebies.'

Andy was not the only person to have seen the bogle. There were others in the village who had seen it, and heard it, too. Indeed, it was getting so bad that nobody would go out after dark at all for fear of meeting the ghost.

That evening, Hamish told Mirren and his mother the story.

'Och, hoots and havers!' said his mother. 'Ghosts and bogles indeed. There's some folk would be daft enough to believe anything.

'But I thought YOU believed in ghosts and Wee Folk,' said Mirren.

'Wee Folk, yes. Anyone with half a brain kens aboot them. But bogles? I've never heard such clishmaclavers. They'll have forgotten about it in a week. You mark my words.'

But the bogle was not forgotten about so easily. And the stories went on until at last Hamish felt he had to find out the truth for himself.

One night, after Mirren and his mother had gone to bed, and wee Torquil was sound asleep in his cradle, Hamish crept out of bed. He tiptoed out of the house in his socks and pulled the door shut behind him. Then he put his boots on and marched off down the road to the ruined cottage.

It was a still black night with not a breath of wind. The moon was a thin slice of silver, and even the stars seemed dull and misty. The only sounds were the soft pad-pad of Hamish's feet on the road and the swish of the grass as he passed.

43

He walked faster and faster. In the darkness the trees and bushes that he knew so well seemed to change shape and to move around him. Hamish was nervous and almost running as he came to the bend in the road that led towards the shore and the old, roofless, ruined cottage. Hunched and black, the empty chimney pointed like a finger to the clouds drifting across the moon.

He held his breath and listened to the silence. There was nothing.

Nothing but his own heart beating softly. Putta-putta-putta. Nothing.

Then suddenly from behind him there came a terrible noise.

Hoooooo-hooooo! Hoooooo-eeeeeech! O-o-o-o-o-h!

Hamish whirled round in time to see a huge white shape flitting through the trees by the cottage. He stepped back and swallowed hard. It was now or never.

'Aye,' he said, lifting his cap. 'It's a fine night for a walk.'

'Hooooooooo – eh?' The white shape stopped whirling and flopped to a halt in front of him. Hamish stepped back and smiled bravely.

'I said it's a fine night for a walk. And

get on, you daft big bogle. I'm no' feared for you.'

The bogle suddenly shot straight backwards, clear through the wall of the cottage, and then trickled back again, like steam from a kettle spout.

'Here, that's a right clever trick,' said Hamish. 'You're no' such a daft big bogle after all. Go on. Let's see you do it again.'

The bogle whirled back to the wall, gathering itself up into a ball of mist. But then instead of going through, it bounced off and fell – flump – like a large untidy bundle of washing, into a clump of nettles.

'Hoooooo-roooooo-eeeeeech!' wailed the bogle.

'Here, I hope you din't hurt yourself, your bogleship,' said Hamish, most concerned.

'It's nae u-u-u-use!' wailed the bogle in a sad, hollow voice. 'You're putting me off. You're supposed to be terrified.'

'Och, I'm sorry,' laughed Hamish. He was beginning to enjoy himself. 'Would it help if I pretended? Here, mind you don't tear your – em – thing.' The bogle was struggling to untangle himself from a bramble bush he had fallen into.

'Ach, but you're no' really feared, are you?' sighed the bogle, with a sob in its voice.

'Well – to be honest, no,' admitted Hamish. 'The way they were talking down at Wee Maggie's I was expecting something really horrible – and you're not that bad.'

'I'm no use at all,' moaned the bogle. 'N-o-o-o u-u-u-use.' His voice was sad as the winter wind. 'I'm just no good at this. I might as well give up and go home. But I haven't got a h-o-o-o-o-me.' He rolled himself up into an untidy ball, groaning and moaning horribly.

'How's that then?' said Hamish. The bogle unwound and wisped himself up a tree.

'Well, it's like this,' he wailed. 'I used to be dead happy, hanging aboot in the old hoose up on the Ben there. I had a great time hurroooing and haunting for aboot three hundred years. But it was an old, old hoose and it just fell tae bits. Naebody would come up and mend it because it was haunted, you see. It got awful cold and windy up there for a poor old bogle . . .'

'So now you're looking for another wee

cottage to haunt?'

'Right you are, pal,' said the bogle. 'I thought this would be just the ticket, but it's just as draughty. That wind's gey cauld some nights. It's no' good for my roo-oo-oo-matissum!' He stretched out and drifted around Hamish like a thin bank of wet fog.

'Right enough, I can see the problem,' said Hamish as the bogle settled in a heap at his feet. 'You have to find somewhere. Look, I tell you what. You just haunt about here for a wee while longer, and I'll see if I can fix you up with something better.'

'Hoooooooo, yir a real pal!' wailed the bogle, vanishing altogether in his excitement.

'Don't mention it,' said Hamish to the empty air. 'I'll be seeing you – wherever you are.'

Next morning, over breakfast, he told Mirren and his old mother the sad story of the bogle.

'He's not coming here,' said his old mother firmly.

'But mother, I thought you didn't believe in bogles!' said Hamish.

'Neither I do. Stuff and rubbish. But

he's still no' coming all the same.' She sniffed and pulled her shawl tighter around her shoulders.

'Och, poor old soul,' said Mirren, who was always kindhearted. 'Maybe he could have a wee corner of the barn.'

'He's no' coming here!' said the old lady, firmly. 'Not even to the barn. The hens would never lay another egg with that thing dreeping in and out.'

Hamish had to agree with her.

'Och, poor old bogle,' said Mirren, spooning porridge into Torquil. 'I suppose there's just nobody has any use for him at all ... Here, just a minute though,' she stopped and smiled. 'I've had an idea.'

The next day Mirren was up early and dressed in her good stout shoes and a warm skirt. She bundled Torquil up and hitched the wee pony to the cart.

'I'm away to see my faither for a day or so,' she said. 'You tell yon bogle no' tae worry. I'll be back soon.'

'Flibbertigibbet!' grumbled the old lady, who was left to wash up the breakfast dishes. But Mirren was away off up the high road to the castle before anyone could stop her.

Mirren's father, the laird, was delighted to see his favourite daughter and even more delighted to see his wee grandson.

'And how are things these days, faither?' Mirren asked when they had settled down over a cup of tea.

'Och, not bad. Not bad. Awful quiet though, Mirren. We're not getting nearly as many tourists round the castle as we used to. Hardly sold a postcard all year. I'm going to have to do something about it, though goodness knows what. But never mind that, my dear, let's hear all your crack.'

So Mirren told her father all the gossip about Hamish, Camusbuie, the farm – and the bogle.

'And I was just thinking, faither, you've some fine big empty rooms in the castle. He could do a rare job haunting them for you.'

'A bogle! In my castle!' The laird was a wee bit taken aback. 'I don't know about that, Mirren. It might put the cook off and, goodness knows, she's bad enough.'

'Och, faither, he wouldn't need to haunt the kitchens. You could have him in the dungeons if you wanted.'

'In the dungeons? Aye – well – maybe,'

the laird stopped and thought about it. 'Here, Mirren, you're brilliant. Maybe that's what the castle needs. A real bogle! My very own haunted dungeon. Noo, there's a thought . . .'

So it came about that the bogle was invited to move into the warm dry dungeon beneath the laird's castle. The laird got a grant from the Tourist Office to put up some new signs and very soon word spread. People came from far and wide to see the haunted dungeon for themselves. The laird organised All-Year-Round Hallowe'en Parties and the bogle had a rare time vanishing in and out through the walls, shaking chains and generally putting on such a

show that everyone went home boasting about how terrified they had been.

Hamish's old mother was right too.

Within a week everyone had forgotten that the old cottage was ever haunted and, in no time at all, Camusbuie went back to being the quiet and peaceful wee village it had always been.

4
Hamish and the Green Mist

It had been a long cold winter. The snow had lain thick on the tops of the hills around Camusbuie for weeks. The burn was a thin trickle of black water between hanging banks of ice, frozen into fantastic shapes. The fields were hard as stone and Hamish had to keep the cows in the byre and feed them on the hay stored through the long days of late summer. He came stamping in from the yard one morning, kicking the snow from his boots, his breath like a dragon's in the cold air.

'Spring's late this year,' he gasped. 'You'd have thought the snow would have begun to melt by now.'

'Aye,' said his mother. 'I don't remember when we had such a long winter.' As if to agree with her, a bank of heavy black clouds rolled down from the top of the Ben. The hillside and trees above the farmhouse vanished in a swirling blizzard.

Week after week it went on. Everyone agreed they had never seen a winter like it. There was no sign of the ground thawing, no chance to plough or dig and plant the seeds for the summer. Down in Camusbuie they could talk of nothing else and, in the freezing air, there was no trace of the soft green mist of the first day of spring.

The old lady listened to Hamish complaining over and over, until at last she had had enough.

'You can sit there and moan until you're blue in the face, Hamish, but I doubt if spring will return until you see to it yourself.'

'See to it myself? What on earth do you mean, mither? You ken fine spring and winter, aye and summer too, come and go on their own.'

'And there's whiles they need a wee bit help, Hamish. I mind fine one winter your father had to do that. He climbed the Ben and I saw neither hide nor hair of him for two days. But when he came back down, the Green Mist followed him and – oh my, but that was a bonny summer.' She put down her knitting and smiled. 'That was the year you were born.'

But Hamish was not listening. He was pulling on his heavy leather jerkin, and climbing into his big boots.

'I'll be back as soon as I can,' he shouted and trudged off, out into the cold.

It was hard work climbing the Ben. The snow had drifted deep and it was as if Hamish was a tiny creature, struggling to cross the soft quilt of a giant's bed. With every footstep, he sank up to the knees.

No longer able to see where he was or find the path, he climbed higher and higher through the thick blizzard. The driving snow lashed his face and there was a great roaring in the air ahead of him. Clinging on with his fingers, he crawled the last few yards to the mountain top and struggled slowly to his feet. The wind seized at him like a ferocious dog tearing at a bone. On the sheet of thick ice his boots were useless and he went flying, head over heels down the frozen slopes of the far side. Over and over he tumbled, round and round, down and down the mountain side, until at last he fell into a thick bank of snow.

The frozen crust crumbled beneath him and Hamish fell, rumbledethump, into a white snow cave around the gnarled roots of an old tree. He rolled over and sat up rubbing his elbow. High above him the wind raged across the hole through which he had fallen.

'You might have warned me you were coming,' grumbled a crotchety voice behind him. Hamish spun round. Bright eyes glittered in the darkness beneath the tree roots. Was it a wolf? Or worse?

'I beg your pardon,' he said. 'I didn't exactly mean to drop in on you like that!'

'Stuff'n'puff!' snarled the crotchety voice again. 'I expect *They* sent you to annoy me. *They're* always at it, the pair of them.' A small man in a very scruffy green suit crawled from a tunnel in the snow and sat cross-legged staring rudely at Hamish.

'Nobody sent me,' said Hamish, brushing himself down. 'I came on my own. And who's "*They*" anyway?'

The little man crossed his arms above his very round stomach, and sniffed rudely.

'Don't tell me you don't know!' he said. 'Or maybe you hadn't noticed there's a war on again.'

'I've no idea what you're talking about,' said Hamish. 'I came up here to try to do something about the winter and . . .'

'That's what I mean,' the wee man squeaked in outrage. 'They're at it again and they don't care who gets in the way. I should have been out of here and down the mountain weeks ago. But here we go again. His High and Mighty Maister of the Ice and the Great Laird of the Gales himself battering away as if nobody else mattered. "I'm the Greatest", "No you're not!".'

The little man hopped around in a fury. 'I'm telling you – whoever you are – their mother should have banged their heads together when they were just wee patches of bad weather!'

'I think I'm beginning to see,' said Hamish. 'It's all their fault. The winter going on like this.'

'You're no' very bright, are you?' said the wee man rudely. 'A right big tumshie. Of course it's all their fault!'

'I'll ignore that,' said Hamish, trying hard to be dignified, 'but how do you stop them fighting?'

'Make them think that somebody's won, I suppose,' said the wee man. 'Though goodness knows how.'

'You mean, if the Master of the Ice thought the Laird of the Gales had won, he'd give up, and . . .

'If the Laird thought the Master of the Ice had won, he'd take a tirl to himself and leave me in peace to get on with the spring weather.'

'Well, there has to be a way,' said Hamish. 'Just let me think about it for a bit.' He curled up in a corner of the snow hole and put his mind to the problem. It was not easy with the wee man sniffing and humphing and grumbling away to himself in the other corner, as he pulled together sticks and dry brushwood to build a fire. Hamish watched him crawl off into the snow tunnels around the tree roots and come back with more bundles of kindling.

'Here!' he grabbed the wee man excitedly by the sleeve. 'I've got it. I've just had an idea.'

'Mind whit ye're at!' squawked the wee man. 'That's an expensive jaicket. An' it's only four hundred year old . . .'

Hamish was hardly listening. He grabbed the bundle of wood and scrabbled around to gather up more.

'As much as you can get!' he shouted.

'I need it all. And help me up out of this hole.'

The wee man moaned and grumbled, but in the end he allowed Hamish to climb up on to his shoulders and passed out the brushwood.

'More! More!' shouted Hamish. 'As much as you can get.' He dragged the wood, slipping and slithering across the ice, staggering against the howling wind, and piled it on the top of the Ben.

Higher and higher the heap grew while the wee man tunnelled beneath the frozen snow hunting for more.

And still the gale howled around Hamish and the ice forming on his hair and eyebrows jingled like tiny bells whenever he shook his head.

At last, when the pile of firewood was the size of a small house, Hamish called to the wee man to stop. He crumpled some dry brown bracken leaves, then took out a box of matches. Shielding them from the gale, he set fire to the bracken and shoved it deep into the heart of the woodpile. The Great Gale, furious at not being able to blow Hamish over, raged around the mountain top. The tiny flames caught up by it, leapt into life and snatched at the sticks, the sticks caught and in no time at all the woodpile was a huge roaring fire, melting the surrounding ice.

The Master of the Ice, feeling a break in his armour, came sweeping back from the north, his deadly breath freezing everything in its path. Far beneath he saw the wind whip the flames until they lit the whole sky and melted the ice cap on top of the Ben of Balvie.

'I have lost,' he wailed. 'I have lost to one greater than I.' The hailstones that swirled around them turned to rain, pitting the melting snow.

Then Hamish turned back to the hole.

'Are you there, wee man? I need green branches, pine and fir. Quickly now. Quickly.' The wee man moaned and grumbled and tunnelled like a whirlwind. Holes appeared in the snow around Hamish, and out shot great branches heavy with sweet-smelling evergreen needles. He seized them and stuck them upright in the soft snow around him.

'Help me, quickly,' shouted Hamish, and the wee man raced around the mountainside sticking the branches in the snow until it seemed as if a tall forest grew there.

The Laird of the Gales, feeling his power broken by the branches, came storming down from the clouds to find a forest growing where none had been. Try though he might to rage and tear at the branches, Hamish and the wee man raced from one to the other, pushing them more and more firmly into the ground as it melted and softened in the heat of the fire. At last the Great Gale died to a whimper.

'I have lost,' he moaned softly. 'I have lost to one greater than I.' The howling winds that raged around him died to a soft and gentle south wind.

As Hamish and the wee man stood and watched, the icicles around them began to drip, drip, drip. At first slowly, and then faster, joining the pools of water on the melting snow.

The clouds above them cleared and a Green Mist rose from the Fairy Glen and crept down the mountainside. Hamish turned to the wee man at his side, but he was no longer there. Rolled up in a green ball, he was trundling down the hillside. As he went, his voice drifted back up.

'Just as well I kent the right thing to

do. Leave it to a big tumshie like yon and naething will ever get done!'

'Well, I like that!' gasped Hamish, then he laughed and looked around him.

Far, far below, a lazy thread of smoke curled up into the clear, blue, windless sky from the chimney of his wee farm-house. He took a deep breath and sniffed the warmth of the first spring air. The white snow-covered fields would soon be ready for ploughing and planting, and the earliest snowdrops would be pushing through the black earth.

'Time for home,' said Hamish. 'There's work to be done.' And, unfastening his heavy leather jacket, he marched off down the mountainside to the farm.

5
Hamish and the Birds

Tap, tap, tap. Tap, tap, tap, went the noise at the window in the very early morning. It woke Hamish from a deep sleep. He stretched and opened one eye to peer out at the grey dawn.

'Too soon to get up,' he said and yawned and snuggled down again.

Tap, tap, tap. Tap, tap, tap, went the noise at the window.

'Hamish,' muttered Mirren sleepily, 'you'll have to trim the branches of that honeysuckle. I've been asking you to do it for weeks.' She turned over and went back to sleep.

Tap, tap, tap. Tap, tap, tap. The noise went on. The more Hamish tried to ignore it, the louder it seemed to become. At last he sighed, climbed out of bed, and padded over to the window.

It was no honeysuckle bush tapping on the glass. It was a bird, the small round robin redbreast, who lived on the farm. For several winters Mirren had given him corn and scraps when she fed the hens, and in spring he had perched at the heel of Hamish's boot as he turned the earth, digging up fresh grubs and worms. The little robin was an old friend of the family.

'What's all the row about,' grumbled Hamish. 'Away back to your nest, you daft wee chookie. There's people trying to sleep in here.' But the robin refused to be chased away. He bobbed up and down bossily on the window-sill, chirping loudly.

'Follow me, follow me.'

'Away you go,' said Hamish. 'I've got more sense. I'm going back to bed. Shoo!' He shut the window firmly, and crawled under the quilt. The little bird was not to be chased away so easily, he fluffed his feathers angrily and went on tapping on the widow pane.

'Follow me, follow me,' he called louder than ever.

'Och, see what he wants, Hamish,' whispered Mirren sleepily.

'Aye – well,' sighed Hamish. 'I suppose there will be no peace in this house until I find out what it is.'

He climbed out of bed, dressed, and went out to find the little bird, perched on a coil of rope in the yard.

'Follow me, follow me,' called the bird.

'I'm coming, I'm coming,' grumbled Hamish, stuffing his shirt into his trousers and pushing his fingers through his untidy ginger hair. The robin fluttered uneasily around the coil of rope, sometimes settling on it, sometimes leaving it to fly around Hamish.

'You want me to bring it along?' he said, picking up the rope.

Scarcely waiting for him, the bird darted out of the garden, along the path between the fields and away from the farm. Hamish staggered behind, trying to loop the rope around his shoulder, tie his bootlaces and keep up at the same time. The robin bobbed from stone to stone on the dusty road. Every now and then he turned to look back and see that Hamish was following.

At the edge of the wood, the robin stopped and sat as if waiting.

'Well, then, what now?' said Hamish. He looked around him. It was quiet and still in the grey early morning, a fine rain had begun to fall and the wind caught the high clouds, tossing them across the sky. He shivered, and scowled at the robin.

'I don't know what I'm doing here,' he grumbled. 'There had better be a good reason or it's no more crumbs for you this winter, I can tell you.'

As they stood glaring at each other, another bird, a young chaffinch, appeared on a branch above their heads. The robin nodded briefly and bossily in his direction, stretched his wings, and flew off back down to the farm. The chaffinch waited to see that Hamish was watching and then, flipping from his branch, flew off into the forest.

'Weet, weet,
Dreep, dreep.'

His cheeky, chirpy voice echoed back through the trees.

'I can see it's weet for myself, thanks,' muttered Hamish pulling his jerkin tight around him. He struggled through the soaking undergrowth of the wet woods, following the bird's song.

'Weet, weet,
Dreep, dreep.'

Showers of raindrops fell from the leaves as the chaffinch fluttered through them, spraying Hamish, soaking his curly hair and running down the back of his collar.

'An' I'll thank you to stop dreeping on

me too!' he shouted. But the chaffinch bobbed on, leading the way.

'Wait for me, will you?' Hamish shouted, then lost his footing and slipped, slithered and tumbled down a muddy slope into a soft, squelching bog.

'Oh – no!' he gasped, hauling himself to his feet. His boots were firmly stuck in the sticky mud.

'I can't go on,' he yelled. 'And if I get out of here I'm going home again. You can sort out whatever it is yourself.' The chaffinch bobbed around his head, chirping loudly.

'I'm telling you, I can't move,' snapped Hamish furiously. 'I'm stuck in the mud! So it's no use you carrying on like that. You'll have to go back and get Mirren. She can pull me out with this rope.'

And it was quite true, the harder he struggled, the deeper his boots sank in the mud.

'Help!' he shouted, 'Help!' But there was no one in the wood to hear him. He pulled, and he heaved, and he shouted louder. And still no one heard him. The chaffinch fluttered around in a panic and then, swooping off, vanished among the trees.

'Fushionless featherbrain!' shouted Hamish, hot and bothered and wrestling helplessly with the mud.

'Loose two boots,' called a calm voice above his head. 'Loose two boots.' He looked up as a large grey pigeon flapped noisily to a landing on an overhanging branch.

'What do you mean?' he demanded. The pigeon cooed softly.

'Loose two boots,
Loose two boots.'

Hamish looked down at his two big feet stuck in the mud.

'Och, I SEE what you mean,' he said and, untying his shoelaces, he stepped out, leaving his boots firmly stuck in the mud. 'All very fine, but here am I in my socks and what happens now?'

'Soon, soon,' promised the pigeon flapping noisily around his head. 'Soon, soon.' He headed off, up the slope.

'Aye – right,' sighed Hamish. 'I suppose I've come this far. I might as well carry on and see what's to do.' He plodded on, feeling his way carefully over the uneven ground in his wet woolly socks, following the crooning pigeon.

'All very well for you, you can fly. My feet are frozen,' he grumbled as he clambered up out of the thick wood, towards the high lonely pine trees.

On a branch above his head, the pigeon waited, watching nervously.

As soon as he saw Hamish leave the trees, the bird spread his soft grey wings and, as if almost afraid to be out of the shelter of his own woods, vanished again among the green leaves.

Hamish stood, alone, at the foot of the rocky slope. Here and there on the way to the summit tall pine trees tossed their tops in the brisk spring wind.

An uncanny, eerie scream rang out, shattering the peace and echoing down the rocky glen. High above his head, gliding on the wind, hung a huge magnificent bird. It swooped down, blotting out the sun for a second, and then soared again, towards the pines. Its weird call rang out, sending other smaller birds hunting for shelter.

The great osprey called again and again and Hamish, hearing the fear in its voice, forgot his wet feet and climbed on, following the bird's vast shadow.

High on the mountainside stood a solitary pine, the tallest – and the last – of the old forest. Ancient as the hillside, it had been the osprey's home for many years. As a child, Hamish had watched, year after year, as the new chicks learned to fly. His father and grandfather before him had made the same climb, to watch the same nest, each summer.

'What ails you?' called Hamish, as the bird swooped and cried repeatedly. And then he heard the frightened voices of the chicks and saw that the old branch on which their nest was built had split in the winter gales and hung limply, swinging loose.

The little cradle of sticks rocked dangerously, like a lifeboat in a storm.

'Wait you now, I'll soon see what can be done,' shouted Hamish. Looping the rope tighter around his shoulder, he wrestled his way up the tree, scraping his hands and face against the rough bark. As he climbed, the tiny chicks weep-weeped in alarm and their huge mother hovered above.

Hamish hauled himself up at last on to a high branch beside the nest, threw the rope across, catching the broken branch, and tied it tightly around the split wood.

'Hold fast,' he shouted, against the

wind that whipped the tree tops. 'Hold fast and I will see what I can do.'

He swung out, dangling dangerously above the drop and, pulling the rope tight, anchored it safely to the tree trunk. Again and again he looped it. At last, when it seemed to him that the nest was firmly wedged, he fastened the rope in three tight knots.

The terrified weep-weep of the chicks instantly became a hungry cry for food. Tiny beaks opened wide as they forgot their fear. The mother bird, seeing Hamish climb back down the tree, settled in the nest to feed them.

Hamish stood beneath the pine tree, watching for a time, to make sure that the nest was quite safe. Then, realising that he too was hungry and had missed his breakfast, he turned to leave.

'I'll bring wee Torquil up to see you next year,' he shouted. 'But I'm thinking by that time you'd do better to build a new nest in a safer place.'

The great mother osprey spread the feather-fingers of her wing-tips wide and circled the sun above his head. Her high joyful whistle of thanks rang out down the glen.

6
Hamish and the Fairy Gifts

With the spring came long soft days and milder evenings. Hamish and Mirren worked hard to dig and plant and sow the seeds that would give them food for themselves and their animals through the summer and the next long winter.

One evening, when the young grass was growing sweet and fresh and the garden around the farmhouse was glowing with daffodils, Hamish stopped to lean over a gate and look around him.

'Aye,' said his old mother from the farmhouse door. 'It's a fine sight. A real credit to you for all your hard work. I think it's high time you had a break and we held a welcome party for wee Torquil.'

Mirren thought it was a wonderful idea, she planned it over tea that night.

'We'll have everyone up from the village, and my father will come – and my sisters . . .'

'Do they have to?' groaned Hamish. Mirren's sisters argued all the time about how fine they were and who had the most money.

'Yes of course we do!' said Mirren, 'And then there's your cousins from over the Ben and everyone from the village. And what about you, mother? Who would you like to ask?'

'Ah well,' said the old lady. She had been waiting for just that moment. 'That's what I was thinking. There's one or two that I think we really OUGHT to invite.' She nodded wisely, winked one eye and tapped the side of her nose. 'You will know who I mean, Hamish.'

'Och, mither!' Hamish sighed, knowing just what she had in mind. 'You can make all sorts of trouble inviting the Wee Folk in. Let's keep it for ourselves.

But his mother was having none of it.

'The Wee Folk were here before us and will still be here long after,' said the old lady firmly. 'Torquil must learn to live with them in peace and, besides, you will see the wonderful gifts they bring. I tell you, Hamish, they must be invited. You just leave it to me. There will be no trouble at all.'

The day of the party grew nearer. The invitations were written and sent out to the family and the people in the village. The old lady went up the hill herself to see the Wee Folk.

Then for weeks on end she and Mirren scrubbed and polished until the house glowed.

From early morning on the day of the party the kitchen was warm with the smell of fresh baking. Every cupboard and table top was piled high with scones, oatcakes and crisp buttery shortbread. Mirren set out cheeses, meat and thick slices of fruit cake. The big black kettle was filled and set to boil by the fireside, and they waited for the guests to arrive.

First to appear was a large farm cart with Mirren's father and her two sisters. Her father, the laird, sat up at the front, chatting happily to the driver, smiling and nodding happily to everyone they passed. Her two sisters, in the back, could be heard arguing even before they crossed the bridge to the farmhouse.

'What do you mean, my dress looks cheap. I can tell you it cost a great deal more than that rag you're wearing.'

'Oh! Is that so, well let me tell you, sister, dear . . .'

'A right pair of greetin' teenies,' grumbled the old lady.

Mirren shook her head, laughing, and

85

went to admire the gifts they had brought for Torquil. Her father gave his grandson a beautiful silver cup. Her sisters had each brought a silver plate. They were furious.

'Why didn't you tell me that's what you were going to give the baby.'

'Well, YOU might have let me know. Mine is finer, anyway. Much more expensive than yours.'

'Oh no it's not!'

'Oh yes it is!'

'We'll ask Mirren which she prefers . . .'

Mirren was fortunately saved by the arrival of a crowd from the village, who came laughing and singing across the bridge to join the party.

Halfway through the afternoon, as she was passing cups of tea around the crowded kitchen, she bumped into Hamish handing out platefuls of cake.

'It's grand, isn't it?' he said, smiling down at her rosy face.

'It is that, and have they not brought some lovely presents for our Wee Torquil?'

The chest by the wall was piled high with soft woollen blankets and clothes for the baby.

'It's all gone very well – so far,' said Hamish. 'And there's no sign of . . .'

'Shhhhhh!' said Mirren. The happy chatter in the kitchen gradually died away and they all stood listening as the wind carried a little tune down the path from the Ben. Torquil, in his cradle, kicked his tiny feet and gurgled happily. The old lady leapt to her feet.

'I knew they would be here,' she said triumphantly, throwing the door open. She stepped out, followed by Hamish, Mirren and the others, to an amazing sight.

Down the path from the Ben came a strange procession. At the head, leading them all, marched a slim figure in a long green cloak and huge shadowy hat. He played on a little golden flute, and his thin fingers danced on the pipe in time to the haunting music. Behind him came a crowd of tiny figures, dressed in green. Some thin, some fat, some young, some old, the Wee Folk skipped, bounced, rolled or flew along the path to the farmhouse.

'Come away, come away,' said the old lady. 'And right glad we are to see you.

Mirren, food for our guests, quickly now.'

Mirren and Hamish fetched out platefuls of meat and cheese, cake and shortbread, and no sooner had they put them down than the Wee Folk, kicking and shoving, had cleared the food and were calling for more.

'Manners like pigs!' sniffed Mirren, but the old lady hushed her with a glance.

'Let them have what they will,' she said 'And let them hear nothing against themselves. Fetch some more cake now.'

So Mirren and Hamish went on carrying out platefuls of food and it did seem strange to Mirren that, however much she carried out, there always seemed to be plenty still in the kitchen. At last it seemed as if the Wee Folk had had enough. They lay around on the grass, laughing and joking, belching and burping rudely. The piper laughed and stepped up to the old lady.

'It is a fine feast you have given us this day,' he said. 'And in return we must honour our pledge of the Fairy Hansel. We would have you take this gift for the child.'

He clapped his hands and two little fat

figures came forward, trundling between them a large, empty, wooden flour barrel. They set it upright in front of the piper, placed the lid on the top and staggered off into the grass, laughing. Hamish and Mirren stared, a strange gift for a new baby, indeed. The man smiled, as if reading their thoughts.

'Strange indeed,' he said. 'But to your son we make the gift of a meal kist that will never be empty so long as he shall live.'

Mirren lifted the lid to find that the barrel, which had been empty, was full to the top with fine white flour.

'Wonderful,' she breathed. 'Our thanks will always be to you and yours . . .'

As she said the words, the procession in front of her dissolved in the air, leaving only an echo of laughter floating on the wind and Mirren and the others gasping in astonishment.

A call from the shore brought them reeling to their senses. They turned to see a small group of figures, dressed in sleek dark clothes, standing on the shingle beach beneath the farmhouse. Their leader held up a hand in greeting.

'The Seal Folk!' said Hamish, recognising the man whom he had cured, and he stepped forward to welcome them. They were happy enough to see him again, but would not come up to his house. Indeed they would not leave the damp sand and stones of the beach between the tides, but they were happy enough to accept a little of the food and drink carried down to them. At last, when they had had enough, their leader held up his hand for silence.

'It is a fine feast you have given us this day,' he said. 'And in return we would have you take this gift for the child.' He clapped his hands and two young men stepped forward, dragging from the water a silver fishing net, as fine as cobweb and sparkling like sunlight. Their leader smiled.

'To your son we make the gift of a fishing net that will never be empty, so long as he shall live.'

Hamish bent to pick up the net, and suddenly found that it was filled with plump silver herring. He laughed and shook his head in amazement.

'How may we ever thank you?'

But the Seal People had already turned back to the sea, wading out and vanishing with hardly a ripple.

'What a wonderful day this is indeed for our Torquil,' said Hamish, turning to his mother. 'It seems that you were right.'

As the old lady smiled and nodded, the air was suddenly shattered by a piercing shriek.

'I know that voice,' Mirren wailed. 'Grizelda Grimithistle!'

Down the road and into the farmyard whirled a green, evil-smelling cloud, that settled slowly to uncover a dirty little witch with spiky hair and a greenish face. It was indeed their old enemy, Grizelda Grimithistle.

'Thought you would invite the Wee Folk to a party and miss out Grizelda, did you?' she screeched. 'We'll soon see about that.'

'Mother!' Hamish was furious. 'I thought you said it would be safe to invite them. You said there would be no trouble.'

'Och, there WILL be no trouble. None at all,' laughed Grizelda. 'I've just come with a wee gift for the bairn. Let's have a look at him.'

Before anyone could stop her she had

pushed forward to the cradle.

'Ach horrible!' she sneered, poking Torquil with a long dirty finger. 'I hate small boys! But I've a present all the same.' She reached down into the pocket of her dirty old coat, took out some green dust and sprinkled it on the baby.

'Here! Stop that!' shouted Mirren, shoving her aside. But it was too late. Grizelda took a deep breath, spread her dirty hands wide and shouted the magic spell.

'Eerie-feerie, tapsalteerie,
Cover his face with – measlie spots!'

'No!' Mirren's horrified shout rang out as Grizelda vanished, leaving only the foul smell behind her. In the cradle Torquil started to wail and rub at the itching red spots that appeared on his face.

'Whit'll we do?' wailed Hamish. 'Mither, don't just stand there. You started this. Do something.'

But for once the old lady was quite at a loss.

Nothing helped. Torquil cried louder and louder and his poor little face under the ginger curls was very soon covered in red measle spots.

93

Mirren picked him up and tried to comfort him. Everyone crowded round with a suggestion.

'Dab the spots with milk!'

'Rub them with butter!'

Suddenly, in the middle of all the fuss, the door swung open and there stood a small round figure.

'The Old Lady from the Ben of Balvie!' said Hamish, stepping forward to meet her.

The little woman was plump, with a rosy face and bright dark eyes. She too was one of the Wee Folk and Hamish had met, and helped her, once a long time ago.

'Indeed,' said the Old Lady. 'I'm sorry to be late for your little party. But it's just as well I came, by the look of it.' She lifted Torquil from Mirren's arms and looked at his scarlet puffy face.

'Poor wee bairn!' she said. 'We'll have to do something about this.' Without another word she turned and marched out of the house and up the path into the woods.

'Here! Come back with our bairn,' shouted Mirren and, followed by the others, she ran after the woman. Up the path she led them, deep into the wood where the birds sang in the tree tops and the flowers bloomed in the grass.

'Wait now, wait,' shouted Hamish's mother, puffing to keep up. But on they went, deeper and darker into the wood. Hamish caught Mirren's hand and pushed on. Leaving the others far behind, they followed the Old Lady until at last she came to a little clearing in the trees and turned to face them. At her feet was a small, perfectly round, dark pool, ringed with strange little yellow flowers, the like of which neither Hamish nor Mirren had ever seen before.

'Now we shall see what can be done for you,' said the Old Lady and she stooped and brushed the baby's face with water from the pool. Then she picked a yellow flower and shook it gently. Torquil stopped crying as the golden pollen dust settled on his face. The Old Lady smiled and sang softly.

'Eerie, feerie, tapsalteerie.
Cover his face with – fairy kisses!'

A golden glow spread around them as she handed Torquil back into Mirren's arms.

'May your wee bairn always live surrounded by love,' she whispered and kissed him gently.

When Hamish's mother and the other party guests finally managed to struggle through the wood to the clearing, they heard the sound of the baby's laughter and found Hamish and Mirren alone with him. Torquil was waving a plump little hand towards the trees. His little round beaming face was covered, not with spots, but with bright golden freckles.

'Well, fancy that!' said Hamish's old mother. 'What was it she did then?'

But Mirren, turning to show her, found that both the pool and the little yellow flowers had vanished. In the quiet wood only the golden evening sunlight glowed on the grass.